APPLEWOOD's
PICTORIAL AMERICA

U.S. CAPITOL
WASHINGTON, D.C.

APPLEWOOD BOOKS
Carlisle, Massachusetts

GROVER CLEVELAND

U.S. CAPITOL
WASHINGTON, D.C.

James Lantos, Editor

Copyright © 2010 Olde Yankee Map and Photo Shoppe

For prints of images in this book visit:
www.pictorialimages.com

Thank you for purchasing an Applewood book.
Applewood reprints America's lively classics —
books from the past that are still of interest to
modern readers. For a free copy of our current
catalog, please write to Applewood Books,
P. O. Box 27, Carlisle, MA 01741.
www.awb.com
www.pictorialamerica.com

ISBN 978-1-60889-024-8

PRINTED IN THE U.S.A.

TABLE OF *Contents*

1790s
p. 4

EARLY 1800s
p. 7

CIVIL WAR PERIOD, 1860–1865
p. 23

LATE 1800s
p. 30

EARLY 1900s
p. 34

MID-LATE 1900s
p. 48

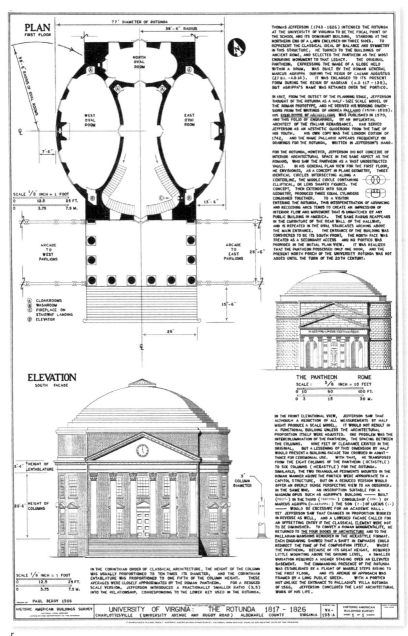

PLAN of the City of WASHINGTON.

Tiber Creek

Reedy Branch

Potomak River

George Town

EASTERN BRANCH

Lat: Capitol 38. 53. N.
Long. ———— 0. 0.

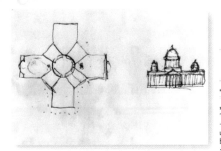

[*N°. 3* AN EARLY SKETCH OF
THE CAPITOL MADE BY
THOMAS JEFFERSON.]

[*N°. 4* AN AD ANNOUNCING
A CONTEST FOR THE
DESIGN OF THE
CAPITOL, 1792.]

{ WASHINGTON, }
{ *In the Territory of Columbia.* }

A PREMIUM,

OF a lot in this city, to be defignated by im-
partial judges, and 500 dollars; or a medal of
that value, at the option of the party, will be
given by the Commiffioners of the Federal Buildings, to the perfon, who, before the 15th day
of July, 1792, fhall produce to them, the moft
approved plan, if adopted by them, for a Capitol to be erected in this City, and 250 dollars,
or a medal, for the plan deemed next in merit
to the one they fhall adopt. The building to
be of brick, and to contain the following apart-
ments, to wit:

A conference room; } Sufficient to ac-
A room for the Re- } commodate 300
   prefentatives; } perfons each.
A lobby, or antichamber to the latter;
A Senate room of 1200 fquare feet area;
An antichamber, or lobby to the laft;

} Thefe rooms to
be of full elevation

12 rooms of 600 fquare feet area, each, for
committee rooms and clerk's offices, to be of
half the elevation of the former. Drawings
will be expected of the ground plats, elevations
of each front, and fections through the building
in fuch directions as may be neceffary to explain
the internal ftructure; and an eftimate of the
cubic feet of brick-work compofing the whole
mafs of the walls.

The Commiffioners.

March 14, 1792.

[*N°. 5* JENKINS HILL, SEEN IN 1792, WAS CHOSEN
AS THE SITE OF THE FUTURE CAPITOL HILL.]

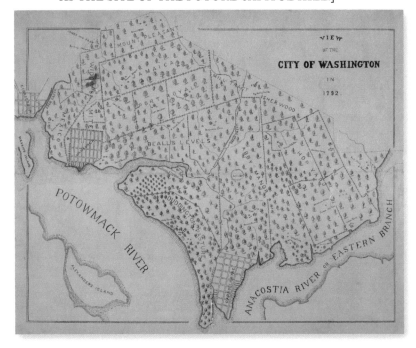

[*N⁰·* 6 GEORGE WASHINGTON LAYING THE CORNERSTONE
IN A MASONIC CEREMONY, SEPTEMBER 18, 1793.]

[*N⁰·* 7 GEORGETOWN AND THE FEDERAL CITY, 1801.]

[*Nos.* 8–9
VIEW OF THE COMPLETED
NORTH (SENATE) WING OF
THE CAPITOL, ca. 1800.]

[*No.* 10　VIEW OF WASHINGTON, 1800.]

[*N⁰·* 11 A DRAWING OF THE CAPITOL BY ARCHITECT
B.H. LATROBE "TO THOMAS JEFFERSON, 1806."]

[*N⁰·* 12 BRITISH SOLDIERS BURNING THE UNFINISHED
CAPITOL, AUGUST 24, 1814.]

BRITISH BURN THE CAPITOL · 1814

[N^o· 13 THE CAPITOL AFTER ITS BURNING.]

[N^o· 14 A DRAWING MADE FROM MEMORY AFTER THE DESTRUCTION
ca. 1814–1820.]

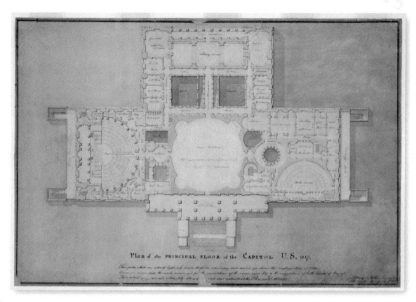

[*Nᵒ·* 15 A NEW PLAN SUBMITTED BY BENJAMIN HENRY LATROBE, 1817.]

[*Nᵒ·* 16 MAP OF WASHINGTON SHOWING THE NEW CAPITOL, 1818.]

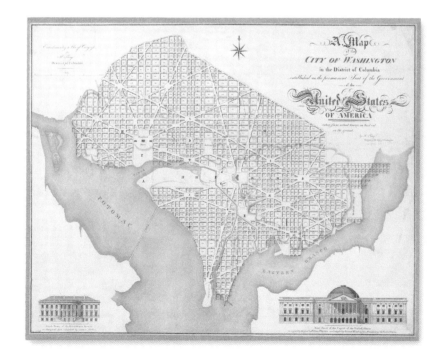

[*N⁰·* 17 THE CAPITOL, 1825.]

[*N⁰·* 18 ANDREW JACKSON TAKING THE OATH OF OFFICE ON
THE EAST PORTICO OF THE CAPITOL, MARCH 4, 1829.]

[*N⁰·* 19 A VIEW OF THE WEST FRONT WITH
COWS IN THE FOREGROUND, 1828.]

[N^o· 20 THE WEST FRONT, FROM CITY HALL, 1832.]

[N^o· 21 WATERCOLOR OF THE EAST FRONT, 1834.]

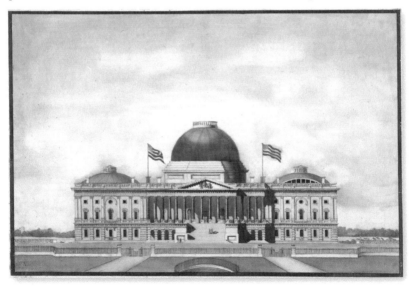

[N^o· 22 VIEW OF THE CITY OF WASHINGTON FROM
BEYOND THE NAVY YARD, ca. 1833–1834.]

$[N^{o.}$ 23 A PRINT BY NATHAN CURRIER, ca. 1835–1836.$]$

$[N^{o.}$ 24 WEST VIEW, 1839.$]$

$[N^{o.}$ 25 VIEW OF WASHINGTON, 1838.$]$

T. Masson.

On stone by F.H Lane.

VIEW OF THE CITY OF WASHINGTON,

THE METROPOLIS OF THE

UNITED STATES OF AMERICA.

TAKEN FROM ARLINGTON HOUSE, THE RESIDENCE OF GEORGE WASHINGTON P. CUSTIS ESQ

[*Nº·* 26 WASHINGTON LOOKING NORTHWEST FROM
SOUTHEAST OF THE CAPITOL, ca. 1846–1855.]

[*Nº·* 27 CURRIER & IVES VIEW FROM
THE PRESIDENT'S HOUSE, 1848.]

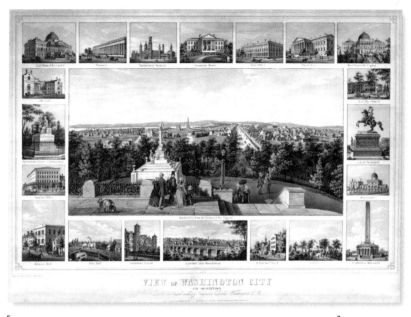

[*N⁰.* 28 WASHINGTON CITY AND GEORGETOWN, 1849.]

[*N⁰.* 29 WASHINGTON, 1850.]

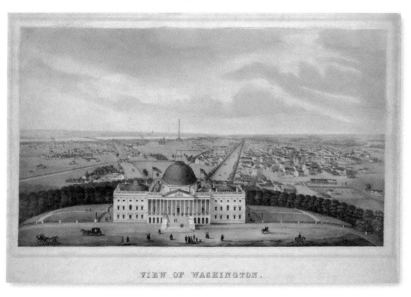

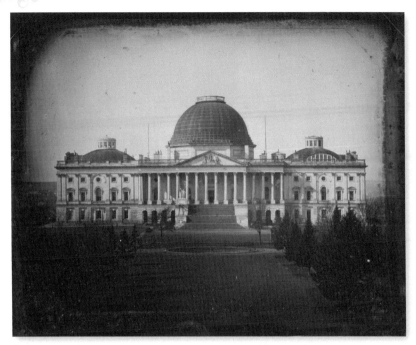

[*N⁰·* 30 DAGUERREOTYPE PHOTOGRAPH, 1846.]

[*N⁰·* 31 THE OLD HOUSE OF REPRESENTATIVES.]

[$N^o.$ 32 THE OLD SENATE CHAMBER, 1850.]

[$N^o.$ 33 VIEW OF THE HOUSE CHAMBER.]

THE HOUSE OF REPRESENTATIVES, U.S. CAPITOL
WASHINGTON, D.C.

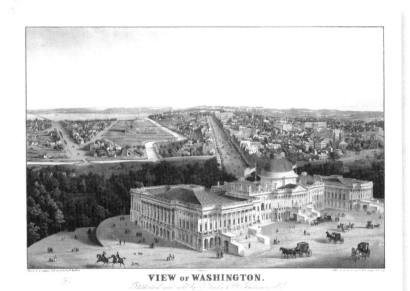

VIEW of WASHINGTON.

[*N⁰.* 34 A PROPOSED DESIGN OF THE NEW CAPITOL, 1852.]

[*N⁰.* 35 ANOTHER PROPOSED VIEW, 1857.]

PANORAMIC VIEW of WASHINGTON CITY.
FROM THE NEW DOME OF THE CAPITOL, LOOKING WEST.

40. PENNSYLVANIA AVENUE AS IT WAS WHEN LINCOLN RODE TO THE CAPITOL FOR
HIS INAUGURATION
Probably never published before

[*N⁰.* 36 "PENNSYLVANIA AVENUE AS IT WAS WHEN
LINCOLN RODE TO THE CAPITOL FOR HIS
INAUGURATION," ca. 1861, WITH THE NEW
CAPITOL DOME UNDER CONSTRUCTION IN
THE DISTANCE.]

[*N⁰.* 37 "INAUGURATION OF MR. LINCOLN, MARCH 4, 1861."]

[*N⁰.* 38   VIEW OF WASHINGTON LOOKING DOWN
PENNSYLVANIA AVENUE, 1860.]
[*N⁰.* 39   CIVIL WAR FUNERAL OF COL. VOSBURGH, JUNE 8, 1861.]

[*N⁰·* 40 RAISING THE FLAG, MAY 1861.]

[*N⁰·* 41 MAP OF GEORGETOWN AND WASHINGTON, 1862.]

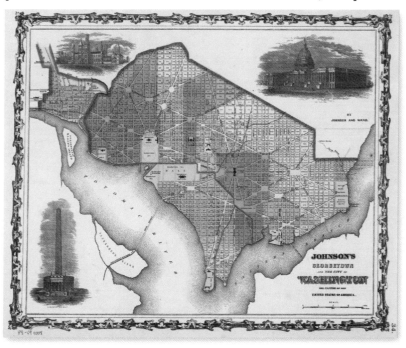

[*N⁰·* 42 ABRAHAM LINCOLN, 1862.]

[*N⁰·* 43 THE STATUE OF FREEDOM ON DISPLAY BEFORE BEING
PLACED ATOP THE NEW CAPITOL DOME, 1863.]

U.S. TROOPS AROUND WASHINGTON CITY, FROM S. TO W

[*Nº* 44 CAMPS OF U.S. TROOPS AROUND WASHINGTON, 1861.]

[*Nº* 45 CAPITOL ROTUNDA DURING THE CIVIL WAR, 1862.]

[*Nº* 46 EARLY PHOTOGRAPH FROM THE CAPITOL LOOKING WEST-SOUTHWEST, 1863.]

[*Nº* 47 DISTRICT OF COLUMBIA & THE SEAT OF WAR, ca. 1860s.]

BIRD'S EYE VIEW OF COLUMBIA AND THE SEAT OF WAR ON THE POTOMAC.

Lithographed and Printed by E. SACHSE & CO., 104 S. Charles St., Baltimore, Md.

Published by C. Bohn, 565 Pennsylvania Avenue, Washington, D. C.

[*Nos.* 48–49 SENATORS & REPRESENTATIVES WHO VOTED "AYE"
TO PROHIBIT SLAVERY IN THE CONSTITUTION, 1864.]

[*No.* 50 "OUR PATRIOTS OF THE WAR," 1864.]

VIEW OF WASHINGTON CITY.

[*N⁰·* 51 CAPITOL VIEW OF WASHINGTON, 1869.]

[*N⁰·* 52 THE CAPITOL, 1882.]

CAPITOL *of the* UNITED STATES
WASHINGTON, D. C.

[*Nᵒˢ·* 53 "THE FLAG THAT HAS WAVED
ONE HUNDRED YEARS," 1876.]

THE FLAG THAT HAS WAVED ONE HUNDRED YEARS.

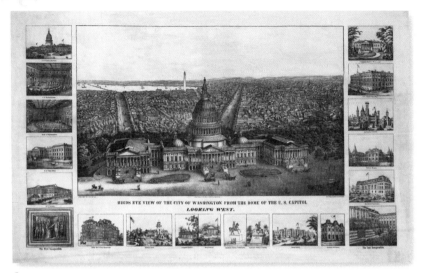

[N⁰· 54 VIEW FROM THE CAPITOL AFTER COMPLETION OF
THE WASHINGTON MONUMENT, ca. 1885.]

[N⁰· 55 HAVERLY'S EUROPEAN MASTODON MINSTRELS, 1898.]

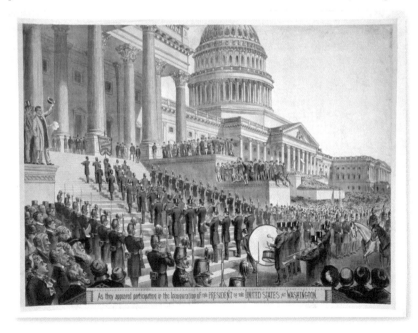

[N⁰· 56 CURRIER & IVES VIEW OF WASHINGTON, 1880.]

THE CITY OF WASHINGTON.

BIRDS EYE VIEW FROM THE POTOMAC-LOOKING NORTH

[*No.* 57 PANORAMIC VIEW LOOKING NORTHWEST
FROM ANACOSTIA, 1901.]

[*N⁰·* 58 CYCLORAMIC VIEW OF THE CAPITOL & CONGRESSIONAL
LIBRARY, 1904.]

51224   THE CAPITOL AT WASHINGTON

[*N⁰. 59* THE CAPITOL, 1902.]

[*N°. 60* **INAUGURATION OF THEODORE ROOSEVELT, 1905.**]

[N°. 61 "SENATE PAGE BOYS STAGE THEIR FIRST SNOW BATTLE
ON THE CAPITOL PLAZA," Early 1900s.]

[N°. 62 PANORAMA OF CAPITOL HILL TAKEN FROM
THE CAPITOL LOOKING EAST, 1909.]

Parade of the G. A. R., 26th Annual Encampment.
WASHINGTON, D. C. SEPTEMBER 20th, 1892.

[N°. 63 PARADE OF THE G.A.R., SEPTEMBER 20, 1892.]

[N°. 64 SNOW SCENE, ca. 1909–1923.]

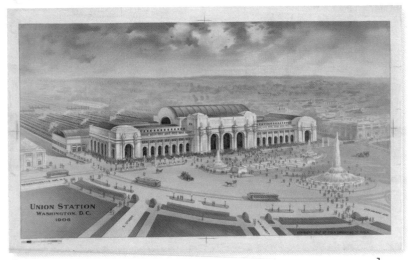

[*NO.* 65 CAPITOL VIEW OF THE NEW UNION STATION, 1906.]

[*NO.* 66 WOMAN SUFFRAGE PROCESSION, 1913.]

[*Nº.* 67 BIRD'S-EYE VIEW OF WASHINGTON, 1916.]

[*Nº.* 68 PLAN FOR THE WASHINGTON MALL AND VICINITY, 1917.]

[*Nº.* 69 GROUP PORTRAIT OF THE SIXTY-FIFTH U.S. CONGRESS, SHOWING JEANNETTE RANKIN, THE FIRST WOMAN ELECTED TO THE HOUSE, ca. 1917–1919.]

[*N⁰.* 70 WORLD WAR I POSTER, 1917.]

[*N°.* 71 WORLD WAR I POSTER, 1918.]

[*N°.* 72 DAYLIGHT-SAVING TIME POSTER, 1918.]

[*N°.* 73 THE CAPITOL AT NIGHT, IN THE RAIN, 1919.]
[*N°.* 74 FIRST SNOW FROM THE STEPS OF THE CAPITOL, 1923.]

[*N°.* 75 AERIAL VIEW OF CAPITOL AND MALL, 1925.]

[*N°.* 76 WARREN HARDING INAUGURATION, 1921.]

[*N°.* 77 FRANKLIN ROOSEVELT INAUGURATION, 1933.]

[*No.* 78 SOCIAL SECURITY PROMOTIONAL POSTER, 1935.]

[*№* 79 TRAVEL ADVERTISEMENT POSTER, 1940.]

[*N°.* 80 DWIGHT EISENHOWER INAUGURATION, 1957.]
[*N°.* 81 CIVIL RIGHTS MARCH, 1959.]

[*N⁰·* 82 PORTRAIT OF NATHANIEL OWINGS, ARCHITECT, 1964.
OWINGS WAS A PRINCPAL CONTRIBUTOR TO THE
REDESIGN OF THE NATIONAL MALL AS WELL AS THE
TRANSFORMATION OF PENNSYLVANIA AVENUE INTO
THE CITY'S GRAND CEREMONIAL BOULEVARD.]

[*N⁰.* 83 THE STATUE OF FREEDOM, REMOVED FOR RENOVATION
IN 1993, THE YEAR THAT MARKED THE 200TH
ANNIVERSARY OF THE LAYING OF THE CORNERSTONE.]

NOTES &
Sources

[Copyright Page] 1888. The Regular Democratic Nominations for President, Grover Cleveland of New York. For Vice Pres't, Allen G. Thurman of Ohio. H.A. Thomas & Wylie lith., New York. Printed by Hojer & Graham, New York.

[Table of Contents] 1973–1974. *L'Enfant (Center) Shows the President His City Plan [1791].* Allyn Cox. Courtesy Architect of the Capitol.

1790s

Page 4. Image No. 1. *University of Virginia, Rotunda, University Avenue & Rugby Road, Charlottesville, Va.* Historic American Buildings Survey.

Page 5. Image No. 2. 1792. *Plan of the City of Washington.* Pierre L'Enfant. Philadelphia.

Page 6. Image No. 3. c. 1790s. *Sketch by Thomas Jefferson for the U.S. Capitol. Washington, D.C.* Library of Congress.

Page 6. Image No. 4. 1792. *Thomas Johnson and Thomas Jefferson [Announcement of Capitol Design Competition].* Philadelphia: *Dunlap's American Daily Advertiser (March 24).* Library of Congress.

Page 6. Image No. 5. 1792. *View of the City of Washington.*

Early 1800s

Page 7. Image No. 6. 1973–1974. *The Capitol's First Cornerstone Laid in September 18, 1793, by President Washington in a Masonic Ceremony.* Courtesy Architect of the Capitol.

Page 7. Image No. 1801. *George Town and Federal City, or City of Washington.* T. Cartwright. London and Philadelphia: Atkins & Nightingale.

Page 8. Image No. 8. c. 1800. *A View of the Capitol of Washington before It Was Burnt Down by the British.* William Russell Birch.

Page 8. Image No. 9. 1973–1974. *North (Senate) Wing of the Capitol in 1800.* Allyn Cox. Courtesy Architect of the Capitol.

Page 8. Image No. 10. 1834. *Washington in 1800.* Boston: Samuel Walker.

Page 9. Image No. 11. 1806. *United States Capitol, Washington, D.C.: Perspective from the Northeast.* Benjamin Henry Latrobe.

Page 9. Image No. 12. 1973–1974. *British Burn the Capitol, August 24, 1814.* Allyn Cox. Courtesy Architect of the Capitol.

Page 10. Image No. 13. 1814. *U.S. Capitol after Burning by the British.* George Munger.

Page 10. Image No. 14. 1814. *U.S. Capitol and Pennsylvania Avenue before 1814.* L. Aikman. Drawing formerly attributed to Latrobe.

Page 11. Image No. 15. 1817. *United States Capitol, Washington, D.C., Principal Floor Plan, Vestibule, Library & Senate Chamber, House of Representatives.* B.H. Latrobe.

Page 11. Image No. 16. 1818. *A Map of the City of Washington in the District of Columbia.* Washington, D.C.:Robert King.

Page 12. Image No. 17. 1825. *Capitol of the U.S. at Washington from the Original Design of the Architect, B.H. Latrobe.* London: Thomas Sutherland.

Page 12. Image No. 18. 1973–1974. *Chief Justice John Marshall Administering the Oath of Office to Andrew Jackson on the East Portico of the U.S. Capitol, March 4, 1829.* Allyn Cox. Courtesy Architect of the Capitol.

Page 13. Image No. 19. 1828. *West Front of the United States Capitol with Cows in the Foreground.* John Rubens Smith.

Page 14. Image No. 20. 1832. *The Capitol—Washington, D.C.—West Front from the City Hall.* Thomas Doughty. Philadelphia: Childs & Inman's Lithographic Press.

Page 14. Image No. 21. 1834. *United States Capitol, Washington, D.C., East Front Elevation.* Alexander Jackson Davis. Rendering.

Page 15. Image No. 22. 1834. *City of Washington from Beyond the Navy Yard.* G. Cooke. Engraved by W.J. Bennett. View, probably 1833, from Anacostia, showing Navy Yard and Capitol in center, Arsenal & White House at left. New York: Lewis P. Clover.

Page 16. Image No. 23. 1835–1836. *Capitol at Washington.* New York: Currier & Ives.

Page 16. Image No. 24. 1839. *Capitol at Washington D.C., West View.* Augustus Kollner.

Page 17. Image No. 25. 1838. *View of the City of Washington, the Metropolis of the United States of America, Taken from Arlington House, the Residence of George Washington.* P. Custis, Esq. P. Anderson del. On stone by Fitz Hugh Lane, Boston. T. Moore's Lithography.

Page 18. Image No. 26. c. 1846–1855. *View of Washington, D.C., Looking Northwest from Southeast of the U.S. Capitol.* Possibly by Augustus Kollner.

Page 18. Image No. 27. 1848. *Washington, from the President's House.* New York: Currier & Ives.

Page 19. Image No. 28. c. 1849. *View of Washington City and Georgetown.* Edward Weber & Co., Baltimore. Washington, D.C.: Casimir Bohn.

Page 19. Image No. 29. 1850. *View of Washington.* Robert Pearsall Smith.

Page 20. Image No. 30. 1846. *United States Capitol, Washington, D.C., East Front Elevation.* John Plumb, photographer. Library of Congress.

Page 20. Image No. 31. 1902. *Scene in the House of Representatives. A Witticism from the Chair.* Published in: "Making Laws at Washington" by Henry Loomis Nelson. *Century,* 64:174.

Page 21. Image No. 32. 1855. *The United States Senate, A.D. 1850.* P.F. Rothermel, drawer; Robert Whitechurch, engraver. Philadelphia: John M. Butler and Alfred Long.

Page 21. Image No. 33. 1866. *The House of Representatives, U.S. Capitol, Washington, D.C.* Baltimore: Edward Sachse & Co.

Page 22. Image No. 34. 1852. *View of Washington.* Edward Sachse. Baltimore: E. Sachse & Co.

Page 22. Image No. 35. 1856. *Panoramic View of Washington City: From the New Dome of the Capitol, Looking West [1857].* Edward Sachse. Baltimore: E. Sachse & Co.

Civil War Period, 1860—1865

Page 23. Image No. 36. 1946. *Pennsylvania Ave., as It Was when Lincoln Rode to the Capitol for His Inauguration.* From "Mr. Lincoln's Camera Man," Meredith.

Page 23. Image No. 37. 1861. *Inauguration of Mr. Lincoln. March 4, 1861.* In album: Benjamin Brown French "Photographs," p. 41. Library of Congress.

Page 24. Image No. 38. 1860. *View of Washington Looking Down Pennsylvania Ave. Toward Unfinished Capitol. National Hotel on Left.* A. Meyer.

Page 24. Image No. 39. May 1861. *Funeral of Col. Vosburgh. The Hearse Approaching the R.R. Depot.* Alfred R. Waud, artist. *New York Illustrated News,* June 8, 1861, p. 77.

Page 25. Image No. 40. 1864. *Raising the Flag, May 1861 (from the original picture by Winner).* Charles Desilver, Philadelphia. William Winner, artist. L.N. Rosenthal, lithographer.

Page 25. Image No. 41. 1862. *Johnson's Georgetown and the City of Washington: The Capital of the United States of America.* New York: Johnson and Ward.

Page 26. Image No. 42. 1862. *Abraham Lincoln.* Boston: Bufford's Publishing House.

Page 26. Image No. 43. January 1863. Freedom *to Surmount the Capitol of United States.* Titian Peale. With backside.

Page 27. Image No. 44. 1861. *Camps of U.S. Troops around Washington City, from S. to W.* Edward Sachse. Washington, D.C.: Casimir Bonn.

Page 27. Image No. 45. 1973–1974. *Rotunda during the Civil War [1862].* Allyn Cox. Courtesy Architect of the Capitol.

Page 27. Image No. 46. 1863. *Early Photographic View of Washington, D.C. from the Capitol Looking West-Southwest.*

Page 28. Image No. 47. 1860s. *District of Columbia and the Seat of War on the Potomac.* Artist, Casimir Bohn, Washington, D.C. Baltimore: E. Sachse & Co., Stephenson, *Cartography of Northern Virginia,* p. 39.

Page 29. Image No. 48. 1865. *Photographs of Senators Who Voted "Aye" on the Resolution Submitting to the Legislatures of the Several States a Proposition to Amend the Constitution of the United States as to Prohibit Slavery.* Portrait: Abraham Lincoln. Powell & Co.

Page 29. Image No. 49. 1865. *Photographs of Representatives Who Voted "Aye" on the Resolution Submitting to the Legislatures of the Several States a Proposition to Amend the Constitution of the United States as to Prohibit Slavery.* Portrait: Speaker Schuyler Colfax. Powell & Co.

Page 29. Image No. 50. 1864. *Our Patriots of the War.* Gaylord Watson.

Late 1800s

Page 30. Image No. 51. 1869. *View of Washington City*. Baltimore: E. Sachse & Co.

Page 30. Image No. 52. 1882. *Capitol of the United States, Washington, D.C.* Buffalo: Courier Lith. Co.

Page 31. No. 53. 1876. *The Flag That Has Waved One Hundred Years—A Scene on the Morning of the Fourth Day of July 1876*. Fabronius, F. P., & L. Restein's oilchromo. Philadelphia: National Chromo Co. Original copyright, J.M. Munyon.

Page 32. Image No. 54. ca. 1885. *Bird's-Eye View of the City of Washington from the Dome of the U.S. Capitol, Looking West*. Baltimore: E. Sachse & Co.

Page 32. Image No. 55. 1898. *Haverly's European Mastodon Minstrels*.

Page 33. Image No. 56. 1880. *The City of Washington: Bird's-Eye View from the Potomac—Looking North*. C.R. Parsons. New York: Currier & Ives.

Early 1900s

Pages 34–35. Image No. 57. 1901. *View Looking Northwest from Anacostia*. John L. Trout. Washington, D.C.: John L. Trout.

Pages 34–35 Image No. 58. 1904. *Cycloramic View of the Capitol and Congressional Library at Washington, D.C.* Frederick W. Mueller.

Pages 36–37. Image No. 59. 1902. *The Capitol at Washington*. Detroit Photographic Co.

Pages 36–37. Image No. 60. 1905. *Inauguration of the President, Washington, D.C.* F.T. Israel.

Page 38. Image No. 61. Early 1900s. *Senate Page Boys Stage Their First Snow Battle on the Capitol Plaza*.

Pages 38–39. Image No. 62. 1909. *Panorama of Capitol Hill, Washington, D.C., Taken from the Capitol Building, Looking East*. Conneaut, Ohio: Haines Photo Co.

Page 39. Image No. 63. 1892. *Parade of the G.A.R., 26th Annual Encampment, Washington, D.C., September 20, 1892*. Geo Prince.

Page 39. Image No. 64. ca. 1909–1923. *Snow Scene, Capitol*. National Photo Co.

Page 40. Image No. 65. 1907. *Union Station, Washington, D.C., 1906*. Philadelphia: Breuker & Kessler Co.

Page 40. Image No. 66. 1913. *Official Program: Woman Suffrage Procession, Washington, D.C., March 3, 1913*.

Page 41. Image No. 67. 1916. *Bird's-Eye View of Washington, D.C.: The Nation's Capital*. H.H. Green, made for the B.S. Reynolds Co. Buffalo: Matthews Northrup Works.

Page 41. Image No. 68. 1917. *Washington, the Mall and Vicinity, Public Buildings Occupied by Various Government Activities, 1917*. Public Buildings Commission. Washington, D.C.: Norris Peters Co.

Pages 40–41. Image No. 69. ca. 1917–1919. *Group Portrait of the Sixty-Fifth U.S. Congress in Front of the U.S. Capitol, Washington, D.C.*

Page 42. Image No. 70. 1917. *United States Official Films Shown Here*. New York: The Hegeman Print.

Page 42. Image No. 72. 1918. *Saving Daylight! Sign and Mail One of These Post Cards to Your Congressman at Washington and Help Make It a National Law to Set the Clock One Hour Ahead.* United Cigar Stores Co.

Page 43. Image No. 71. 1918. *"I Summon You to Comradeship in the Red Cross" - Woodrow Wilson/Harrison Fisher.* New York: American Lithographic Co.

Page 44. Image No. 73. 1919. *View of the U.S. Capitol, at Night, in Rain.* Photo by Grenbeaux.

Page 44. Image No. 74. 1923. *The First Snow in the National Capitol—Scene from the Steps of the U.S. Capitol, Looking toward the Congressional Library.* February 6, 1923. National Photo Co.

Page 45. Image No. 75. 1925. *Aerial View of the Capitol and Mall, Washington, D.C.*

Page 45. Image No. 76. 1921. *Harding Inauguration, March 4, 1921.* Harris and Ewing. Schutz Group Photographers.

Page 45. Image No. 77. 1933. *Aerial View of U.S. Capitol and Crowd on the Grounds of the East Front of the U.S. Capitol, during the Inauguration of Franklin Delano Roosevelt, March 4, 1933.* Courtesy Architect of the Capitol.

Page 46. Image No. 78. 1935. *A Monthly Check to You for the Rest of Your Life, Beginning When You Are 65.* Newman. Washington, D.C. Social Security Board.

Page 47. Image No. 79. c. 1940. *Pennsylvania Railroad—Washington, the City Beautiful.* Grif Teller. Clifton, N.J.: Osborne Co.

Mid-Late 1900s

Page 48. Image No. 80. 1955. *President Dwight D. Eisenhower Delivering His Inaugural Address on the East Portico of the U.S. Capitol, January 21, 1957.* Courtesy Architect of the Capitol, Library of Congress.

Page 48. Image No. 81. *More than 15,000 White and Colored Persons Met Here 4/18 on Behalf of School Integration and Civil Rights Legislation.* April 18, 1959. United Press International Telephoto. *New York World-Telegram.*

Page 49. Image No. 82. 1964. *Portrait of Nathaniel Owings.* Courtesy of Vincent Perez, artist.

Page 50. Image No. 83. 1993. *U.S. Capitol, Statue of Freedom.* On May 9, 1993, the statue was removed from its pedestal by helicopter for restoration. Historic American Buildings Survey.

Many images in this book come from the collections at the Library of Congress.

CPSIA information can be obtained at www.ICGtesting.com
Printed in the USA
BVIW12n2238080517
483571BV00004B/12